£2

# What Game Shall We Play?

## PAT HUTCHINS

JM Julia MacRae Books
A DIVISION OF WALKER BOOKS

So off they went to look for Fox.
Duck looked across the fields,
but he wasn't there.

Frog looked among the tall grass,

So off they went to look for Mouse.
Duck looked over the wall,
but Mouse wasn't there.
Frog looked under the wall,
but she wasn't there, either.

So Fox looked in the wall,

and there he was.

"What game shall we play, Rabbit?"
they asked.
"I don't know," said Rabbit.
"Let's go and ask Squirrel."

So off they went to look for Squirrel.
Duck looked behind the tree,
Frog looked in front of the tree,
Fox looked up to the top of the tree,
Mouse looked under the tree,

and Rabbit looked
through the leaves
of the tree,

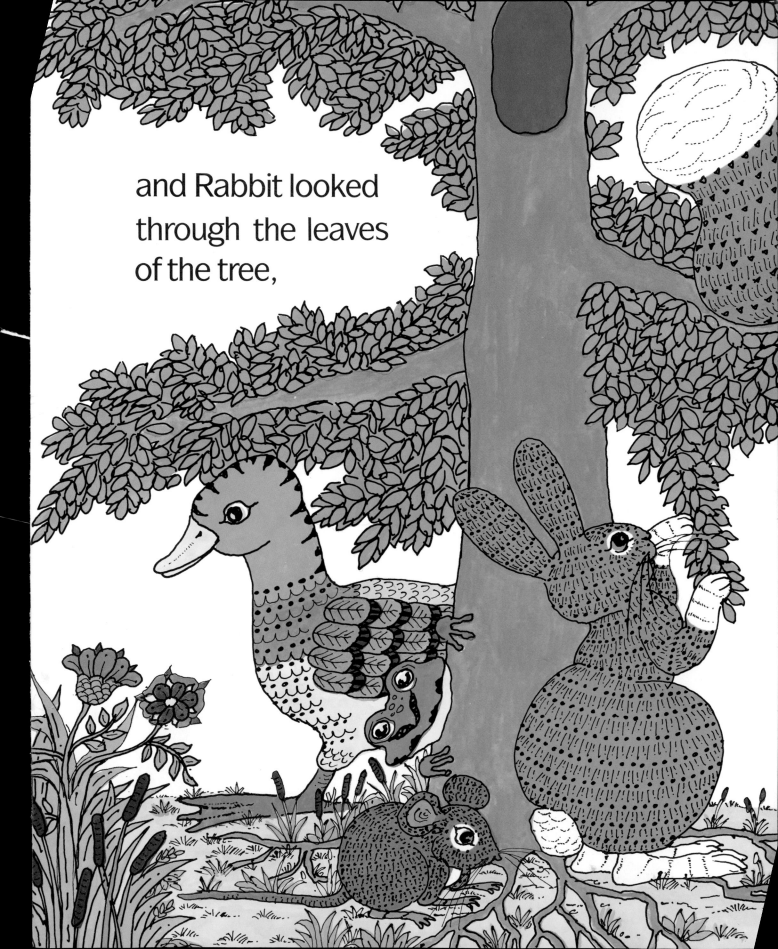

and there she was.

"What game shall we play, Squirrel?"
 they asked.
"I don't know," said Squirrel.
"Let's find Owl and ask him."

But Owl found them first.
"What game shall we play, Owl?"
they asked.
"Hide and seek," said Owl.

And while Owl closed his eyes,
Duck and Frog hid in the pond,
Fox hid in the long grass,
Mouse hid in the wall,
Rabbit hid in the hole,
and Squirrel hid in the leaves in the tree.

Then Owl went to look for them.